The Tyger Voyage

by Richard Adams

illustrated by Nicola Bayley

JONATHAN CAPE

THIRTY BEDFORD SQUARE

LONDON

For Katharine

FIRST PUBLISHED 1976
TEXT © 1976 BY RICHARD ADAMS
ILLUSTRATIONS © 1976 BY NICOLA BAYLEY

JONATHAN CAPE LTD
30 BEDFORD SQUARE, LONDON WCI

ISBN 0 224 01237 1

PRINTED IN ITALY BY A. MONDADORI EDITORE, VERONA

My father's got some curious friends —
   At least, I s'pose it all depends
On what you mean by curious —
   But some are not at all like us.

He takes a friendly interest
   In neighbouring bird and local beast.
The Dubbs live just across the way.
   (The Dubbs are tygers, I may say.)

One night last year, across the port,
   He sat some time in silent thought.
At last he said, ''Whatever next?
   I don't know when I've been so vexed.

[4]

"James Price was saying at the club
    Ezekiel and young Raphael Dubb
Have bought a boat and seriously
    Intend to take the thing to sea."

For days my father, muttering
    "Most dangerous — not at all the thing —
Price says it's nothing but a tub — "
    Failed to dissuade Ezekiel Dubb.

Well, we assembled with the rest
    (My father under strong protest)
To cheer them off at morning light
    And wave till they were out of sight.

[6]

The weeks passed; not a postcard came.
  My father felt himself to blame.
No news of shipwreck or mishap:
  They'd simply vanished off the map.

What follows now is what we learned
  Much later, when the Dubbs returned.
I think it only goes to show
  With tygers, that you never know.

They sailed away, the wind blew high,
  All round them naught but sea and sky.
And day and night, while Raphael steered,
  Strange dawns
              and stranger stars appeared.

[8]

Then came a sudden stormy day
    With toppling waves and ice-cold spray,
And when night fell the bleak moon shone
    On broken masts and compass gone.

They drifted, full of fear and doubt,
    And late next afternoon made out
A distant coastline, fringed with trees,
    That rose and fell between the seas.

The storm wind dropped,
                the shore was reached,
    The battered vessel safely beached.
There stretched away, on either hand,
    An empty and unpeopled land.

For days, till all their food was gone,
　Through woods and swamps
　　　　　they struggled on,
Crossing on rafts the muddy lakes
　Infested with bright water-snakes.

Seeking one day a place to camp
　Above the forest's gloomy damp,
Ezekiel crossed a ridge of sand,
　And saw the mountain close at hand.

Ezekiel climbed the rocks in hope
　While Raphael brought the telescope.
Beyond dense forests they descry
　A mountain, smoking to the sky.

[12]

It seemed to him that from that height
　　Some road or town might be in sight.
And Raphael, hungry, thought that they
　　Should start the ascent without delay.

As they set out, a mountain fox
　　Came slinking towards them
　　　　　　　through the rocks
And at a distance, from the scrub,
　　Barked sharply to Ezekiel Dubb.

"It's seven years I've known this range.
　　There's something wrong —
　　　　　　some threat, some change!
I'd keep away — don't ask me why."
　　The Dubbs pushed on without reply.

[14]

The climb was arduous and slow.
    They cut steep steps across the snow,
And, peering down
                    through cloud-wrack, saw
    Far, far below, the swamp-lake's shore.

Still upwards in a drifting smother,
    They clambered one behind the other,
And as they crossed the ice-cracks deep
    The mountain muttered in its sleep.

At last they reached the topmost ledge
    Upon the very crater's edge.
Ezekiel, from an oilskin bag,
    Unwrapped and flew the Tyger Flag.

Cheering above that frightful drop,
    They stood upon the mountain top,
All in a strange and breathless gloom
    Of mist and snow and sulphur fume.

And then a swift, instinctive sense,
    Some trembling dread,
                made Raphael tense,
Warned, as though by an unseen stranger,
    Of imminent and fearful danger.

Down, down, each minute like a day,
    Ezekiel, panting, led the way.
The sun grew dark, and all around
    A bitter dust fell on the ground.

Sliding and stumbling down the rock,
    They felt the first eruption-shock,
As from the mountain's peak there came
    A horrid and malicious flame.

Far down the mountain's further side
    They found a cave in which to hide,
And half the night, as in a dream,
    They watched the glowing lava stream.

Next day they saw, on venturing out,
    Pumice and ashes all about.
Raphael was feverish and faint
    But staggered on without complaint.

Dusk found them on a lonely track,
  Ezekiel carrying Raphael's pack,
And as they lay in desperate plight
  Three gypsy-wagons came in sight.

The silent gypsies took them in,
  Exhausted, lost, half-starved and thin;
And Raphael Dubb they put to bed,
  For he was wandering in the head.

And as they rode through uplands steep
  An old, wise woman watched his sleep.
Strange herbal remedies she blended,
  And slowly Raphael's health amended.

Meanwhile Ezekiel set to learn
    The skills by which all gypsies earn —
Or do not earn — their food and keep.
    He made good clothes-pegs, very cheap;

Went poaching with the Romany Chal
    And read the Tarot magical.
And so like gypsies, lean and tanned,
    They travelled on from land to land.

It's always been my father's way
    To take an autumn holiday;
To go abroad and stay a space
    In some secluded watering-place.

[24]

One day, approached outside the shops
    By fellows selling pegs and props,
He murmured some appropriate snub
    And recognized — Ezekiel Dubb!

Though shocked,
        he still found words of cheer.
    "Dear chap, how nice to meet you here!
Er — let us send a telegram.
    Most glad to see you — really am."

Although the gypsies made a fuss
    My father was impervious.
The Dubbs, protesting all in vain,
    Were put on board the Paris train.

From there it was a trifling step
    To reach Newhaven via Dieppe.
(Young Raphael, to my father's grief,
    Retained his gypsy handkerchief.)

See, they are home, now bang the drum!
    The Mayor and Corporation come!
A Civic Dinner, wine and beef.
    (Oh dear, oh dear — that handkerchief!)

Raphael's requested me to write
    Their story down in black and white.
It's his idea to print a few
    To circulate to friends like you.

[28]

My father's read this tale I've told
    Of noble deeds and travels bold.
He says that while he must admit
    The pair showed admirable grit,
He thinks that I should emphasize
    Their trip was really *most* unwise.

[30]